the BIG worry day

by K. A. Reynolds

illustrated by Chloe Dominique

VIKING

I have a dog named Bea.
She worries. Like me.

This morning, Bea wakes me up, nervous
about all that we have to do today.

Even though it's the weekend
and the only thing on our agenda is:
go outside and play.

Bea pokes her head inside the covers
and gives me a worried look.
So many bad things could happen outside.

Bea looks worried that we might get cold.

"Don't worry, Bea. I'll bring our sweaters."

Now Bea looks worried that we might get lost.

"I know. I'll bring a compass and all my maps."

Bea looks worried that we might get hurt running around outside.

"We should bring a first aid kit, just in case."

Bea doesn't know what she'll do if she runs into monsters . . .

"We should definitely bring our swords."

Even with all my suggestions,
Bea is still worried.
How do I help her feel calm?

I think I know just what to do.

We take deep, relaxing breaths,
one after the next,

and imagine our most favorite things.

We do yoga with friends to unwind.

I like some poses more than others.

But Bea loves Downward Dog best.

We write down what scares us most
and share our fears with the group.
When some of us get emotional,
we take turns hugging it out.

Then, when Bea's finally feeling calm,
I rub her belly until she smiles . . .

and shows me
she's ready to go.

After a few deep breaths,

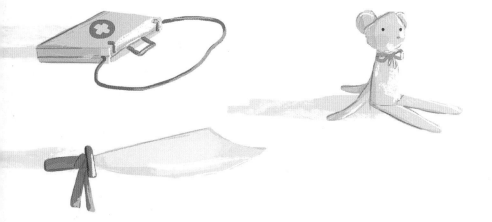

Bea thinks maybe we don't need
so many things to feel safe.

But bringing one thing might be nice.

Because I know what it's like
to want to go into the world on adventures
and hide in your room at the same time,

we bring just a bit of home with us.

So we can relax and enjoy the day.

Author's Note

Life is unpredictable. And for a child with anxiety, this unpredictability can be debilitating. One of my earliest memories revolves around my anxiety. I was four years old. I'd just climbed into my beloved little blue wagon and was doing what I always did: stretching out my legs, ready to go. But suddenly . . . my legs wouldn't lay flat. My worries spun out of control. If I could grow too big for my wagon, what *else* would change if I kept growing? Would my favorite clothes not fit? Would I get too big for my bed? My shoes? Would I be too big to hold? Anxiety pulled my mind in a million different directions. Too many to manage on my own. I worried about this so much, I made a wish right then to stay four years old forever. I grew regardless, of course. And my anxiety grew with me.

As a child living with undiagnosed general and social anxiety, my worries would get so big, the thought of a sleepover, swim, or playing outside filled me with such dread, I'd have much rather stayed home. Where it was safe. Predictable. Where I knew what would happen next. My worries felt like stop signs in front of me—not only blocking me from trying new things, but stopping me from enjoying my favorite things, too. And because my anxiety went undiagnosed, the adults in my life didn't know what to look for to help me.

They didn't see that my inability to relax was clinical. That my fears about safety—for myself, friends, and family—were out of the ordinary. They didn't understand my perfectionism, need for order, and daily stomachaches. They didn't realize that my worrying about things before they happened, and lack of focus, stemmed from mental illness. So going forward into adulthood, I had to learn to cope with my anxiety by myself.

And that made me feel so alone.

Still, as an adult, I managed to find some healthy coping mechanisms for my anxiety. Devices like breathing deeply when I feel panic and worry coming on. Or imagining the very thing I'm worried about inside a big bubble and envisioning myself blowing it away. Sometimes listening to music helps me relax. Or sitting quietly outside. Reading poetry, practicing yoga, and doing meditation can also soothe my racing mind. And of course, I love hanging out with my big goofy dogs! More often than not, all of these exercises help calm me and get me to a place where I can feel safe in my body and environment enough to enjoy this beautiful world. And maybe, in addition to these practices, you'll find even more wonderful ways to help your anxiety, too.

I wrote *The Big Worry Day* to show children living with anxiety (and maybe even some adults!) that with a bit of preparation, imagination, self-care, and a little help from their furry and non-furry friends, they can help themselves feel safe in their world. That they can have fun, even with anxiety. I wanted to show that we are more than our worries and fears. We are loving and loved, and in this together. And above all else, we are not alone.

If you'd like to read more children's books that revolve around anxiety and ways to manage it, these are some others I think you might enjoy:

Breathe Like a Bear by Kira Willey, illustrated by Anni Betts
I Am Yoga by Susan Verde, illustrated by Peter H. Reynolds
A Handful of Quiet by Thich Nhat Hanh, illustrated by Wietske Vriezen
Sitting Still Like a Frog by Eline Snel

For the dogs: The barkers, jumpers, and diggers. The farting, cuddling, tear-lickers. The "Gah! I just made that sandwich!" thieves who steal our lunches and our hearts. (And to Eugene, Phoebe, Louie, Chester, Marseline, and Sherman. For the infinite gift of your love, and for showing me the way.) —K. A. R.

For the friends who help make our worries smaller, and the worriers who are braver than they think. And a special thank-you to Loki and Gavin, who are always ready for adventure. —C. D.

VIKING

An imprint of Penguin Random House LLC, New York

First published in the United States of America by Viking, an imprint of Penguin Random House LLC, 2022

Text copyright © 2022 by K. A. Reynolds
Illustrations copyright © 2022 by Chloe Dominique

Visit us online at penguinrandomhouse.com.

Library of Congress Cataloging-in-Publication Data is available.

Manufactured in China

ISBN 9780593465639

1 3 5 7 9 10 8 6 4 2

TOPL

Design by Kate Renner
Text set in ITC Mendoza Roman

The artwork for this book was created digitally using pencil and paintbrushes in Procreate and Photoshop.

Note: This book is intended to provide helpful and informative material on the subject matter covered. Please practice yoga safely and with an adult.